Enid Blyton

The
Little Yellow Bird

& The Lambikin

Illustrated by RENE CLOKE

DERRYDALE BOOKS
NEW YORK

THE LITTLE YELLOW BIRD

There was once a little bird who loved cheese. He thought it was far, far nicer than butter, and if he could steal some, he would!

He flew into the grocer's shop and pecked a big hole in the cheese there.

He sat on Mrs.
Tippy's shopping
basket as she went
home, and pecked a
big piece out of her bit of cheese too.

And do you know, he even went into
Old Man Dingle's garden and pecked the
tiny bits of cheese out of the mouse-traps,
he had set there to catch mice who ate
his peas! Wasn't he a thief?

He ate so much cheese
that he grew quite yellow,
and people began to call him
the cheese-bird.

They thought he was a
greedy little thing, and if
ever he came to tea with
them, they made sure not to
have any cheese, for if they
did he would eat up every scrap.

So, when he popped into their houses,
and they offered him bread and butter, or
bread and jam, he would put his head on
one side, look down his beak in
a very haughty manner, and say:
"What! No cheese!"

He went to tea with Mrs. Frilly, and
she gave him egg sandwiches. "What!
No cheese!" he cried, and wouldn't eat a
thing.

He went to supper with Dickory Dock,
who had got a nice meal of sardines and cocoa ready.

"What! No cheese!"
cried the greedy bird,
and he wouldn't touch
anything at all.

It seemed such a waste of a meal,
because Dickory Dock couldn't possibly
eat it all himself.

One day the pixie Long Legs gave a fine
party. There were strawberries and
cream, vanilla ices and lemonade, and you
would have thought
anyone would have
been pleased,
wouldn't you?

But the little yellow bird turned up his
beak at everything. "What! No cheese!"
he cried again.

Long Legs was angry. "No," she said,
"there isn't any cheese, you greedy little bird."

"Who stole cheese from
the grocer? Who stole
Old Man Dingle's mouse-trap
cheese? Go away, you greedy thing – and
don't come back here again! Sing a song
about cheese if you want to – *we* won't listen."

So the little bird
had to fly away
into our world.
There he found that
people were as kind as
could be and put out crumbs
and potato and coconut and fat – but,
of course, not a scrap of cheese!

And so all day
long he sits on the tele-
graph wires, or on a high
hedge, and sings the same
little song over and over again.
"Little bit of bread but no CHEESE!
Little bit of bread but no CHEESE!
Little bit of bread but no CHEESE!"

Have you heard him? He is singing it
this summer just as usual, for I've heard
him three times
already to-day.

We call him the
yellow-hammer and he is a bird
rather like a sparrow, but yellow...and
dear me, how he sings his little song -
"Little bit of bread but no CHEESE!"
Do see if you can hear him. He sings
it as plainly as anything.

THE LAMBIKIN

There was once a Lambikin
who frolicked about and
had a lovely time. One day he
set off to visit his Granny. He
frisked along, thinking of all the
lovely things she would give
him, when he
met a Jackal.

"Hey, Lambikin,
stop!
I'll EAT you!"
cried the Jackal.
But the Lambikin
jumbed high into

the air and cried:
"To my Granny's house I go,
and I shall fatter grow,
then you can eat me so."

"Very well," said the Jackal,
and he let the Lambikin go on his
way. Soon he met a Vulture, who
shouted to the Lambikin:
"Hey, Lambikin, stop! I'll
EAT you!"

But the Lambikin frisked round
him and laughed:

"To my Granny's house I go,
and I shall fatter grow,
then you can eat me so!"

"Very well," said the
Vulture, and he let the
Lambikin go on his way.

Presently he met
a Tiger, who called:
"Hey, Lambikin,
stop! I'll
EAT you!"

But the Lambikin
jumped about on his
four frisky legs and cried:
"To my Granny's house I go,
and I shall fatter grow,
then you can eat me so."

"Very well," said the Tiger,
and he let the Lambikin go on his
way. Soon the little creature came
to his Granny's house and greeted
her with joy.

"Granny," he said, "I've pro-
mised to get fat. So will you
please put me in the corn-bin?"

His Granny
popped him in
there and he
ate for seven
days till he
could eat no more.

"Granny," he said,
when he came out,
"I am so fat now
that I am afraid I
shall be eaten on
my way home.
Please make a
drumikin for me,
and put me inside."

So his Granny
made a drumikin
for him out of a
barrel with skin
stretched over each end, and he set
off home rolling along inside the
drumikin.

Soon he met the Tiger,
who called out: "Drumikin,
drumikin, have you seen Lambikin?"
"He's lost in the forest and so are you.
On, little drumikin! Tum-pa, tum-poo!"
cried Lambikin.

"What a pity!"
said the Tiger, and
let the drumikin roll
on its way.

Soon the Vulture flew down,
and cried: "Drumikin, drumikin, have you seen Lambikin?"
"He's lost in the forest and so are you.
On, little drumikin! Tum-pa, tum-poo!"
cried Lambikin.

"What a pity!" said the Vulture and let the drumikin roll on
its way.

Soon the Jackal
came up and cried:
"Drumikin, drumi-
kin, have you seen Lambikin?"

"He's lost in the forest and so are you.
On, little drumikin! Tum-pa, tum-poo!"
Cried Lambikin.

    But the Jackal knew Lambikin's
voice and rushed after the drumikin. In a fright the Lambikin
rolled the drumikin down the hill
to his home with the Jackal close
after him.
He bumped open the door of his
house and got inside just in time.
"Tum-pa, tum-poo!" he cried!